PIPPI GOES TO THE CIRCUS

by Astrid Lindgren
pictures by Michael Chesworth

PUFFIN BOOKS

Way out at the end of a tiny little town was an old overgrown garden, and in the garden was an old house, and in the house lived Pippi Longstocking. She was nine years old, and she lived there all alone. She had no mother and no father, and that was of course very nice because there was no one to tell her to go to bed just when she was having the most fun, and no one who could make her take cod liver oil when she much preferred caramel candy.

Once upon a time Pippi had had a father of whom she was extremely fond. He was a sea captain who sailed on the great ocean, and Pippi had sailed with him in his ship until one day her father was blown overboard in a storm and disappeared. But Pippi was absolutely certain he would come back.

Her father had bought the old house in the garden many years ago. While Pippi was waiting for him to come back she went straight home to live at Villa Villekulla. That was the name of the house.

Two things Pippi took with her from the ship: a little monkey whose name was Mr. Nilsson—he was a present from her father—and a big suitcase full of gold pieces. Pippi also had a horse of her own that she had bought with one of her many gold pieces the day she came home to Villa Villekulla.

Beside Villa Villekulla was another garden and another house. In that house lived a father and mother and two charming children, Tommy and Annika, who often wished for a playmate. And when Pippi Longstocking moved next door, they got the best playmate any child could wish for. This is the story of one of their adventures together. . . .

A circus had come to the little town of Ville-kulla, and all the children were begging their mothers and fathers for permission to go. Of course Tommy and Annika asked to go too, and their kind father immediately gave them some money.

Clutching it tightly in their hands, they rushed over to Pippi's. She was on the porch with her horse, braiding his tail into tiny pigtails and tying each one with red ribbon.

"I think it's his birthday today," she announced, "so he has to be all dressed up."

"Pippi," said Tommy, all out of breath because they had been running so fast, "Pippi, do you want to go with us to the circus?"

"I can go with you most anywhere," answered
Pippi, "but whether I can go to the surkus or not I
don't know, because I don't know what a surkus is.
Does it hurt?"

"Silly!" said Tommy. "Of course it doesn't hurt; it's
fun. Horses and clowns and pretty ladies that walk
the tightrope."

"But it costs money," said Annika, opening her
small fist to see if the shiny half-dollar and the quar-
ters were still there.

"I'm rich as a troll," said Pippi, "so I guess I can
buy a surkus all right. But it'll be crowded here if I
have more horses. The clowns and the pretty ladies I

could keep in the laundry, but it's harder to know what to do with the horses."

"Oh, don't be so silly," said Tommy, "you don't buy a circus. It costs money to go and look at it—see?"

"Preserve us!" cried Pippi and shut her eyes tightly. "It costs money to *look*? And here I go around goggling all day long. Goodness knows how much money I've goggled up already!"

Then, little by little, she opened one eye very carefully, and it rolled round and round in her head. "Cost what it may," she said, "I must take a look!"

At last Tommy and Annika managed to explain to Pippi what a circus really was, and off they all went.

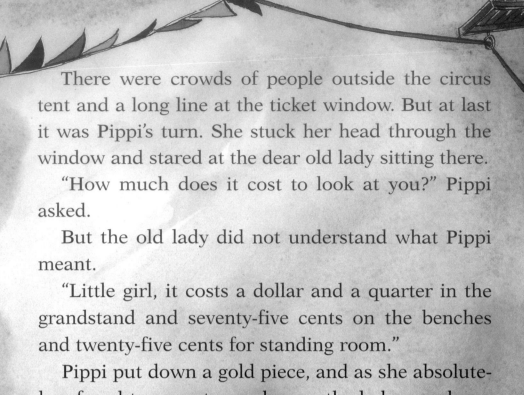

There were crowds of people outside the circus tent and a long line at the ticket window. But at last it was Pippi's turn. She stuck her head through the window and stared at the dear old lady sitting there.

"How much does it cost to look at you?" Pippi asked.

But the old lady did not understand what Pippi meant.

"Little girl, it costs a dollar and a quarter in the grandstand and seventy-five cents on the benches and twenty-five cents for standing room."

Pippi put down a gold piece, and as she absolutely refused to accept any change, the lady gave her a

ticket for the grandstand and gave Tommy and Annika grandstand tickets too without their having to pay a single penny. In that way Pippi, Tommy, and Annika came to sit on some beautiful red chairs right next to the ring. Tommy and Annika turned around several times to wave to their schoolmates, who were sitting much farther away.

"This is a remarkable place," said Pippi, looking around in astonishment. On a platform nearby the circus band suddenly began to play a thundering march. Pippi clapped her hands wildly and jumped

up and down with delight.

"Does it cost money to hear too?" she asked. "Or can you do that for nothing?"

At that moment the curtain in front of the performers' entrance was drawn aside, and the ringmaster in a black frock coat, with a whip in his hand, came running in, followed by ten white horses with red plumes on their heads.

The ringmaster cracked his whip, and all the horses galloped around the ring. Then he cracked it again, and all the horses stood still with their front feet up on the railing around the ring.

One of them had stopped directly in front of the children. Annika didn't like to have a horse so near her and drew back in her chair as far as she could, but Pippi leaned forward and took the horse's right foot in her hands.

"Hello, there," she said, "my horse sent you his best wishes. It's his birthday today too, but he has bows on his tail instead of on his head."

Luckily she dropped the foot before the ringmaster cracked his whip again, because then all the horses jumped away from the railing and began to run around the ring.

When the act was over, the ringmaster bowed politely and the horses ran out. In an instant the curtain opened again for a coal-black horse. On its back stood a beautiful lady dressed in green silk tights. The program said her name was Miss Carmencita.

The horse trotted around in the sawdust, and Miss Carmencita stood calmly on his back and smiled. But then something happened; just as the horse passed Pippi's seat, something

came swishing through the air—and it was none other than Pippi herself. And there she stood on the horse's back, behind Miss Carmencita. At first Miss Carmencita was so astonished that she nearly fell off the horse. Then she got mad. She began to strike out with her hands behind her back to make Pippi jump off. But that didn't work.

"Take it easy," said Pippi. "Do you think you're the only one who can have any fun? Other people have paid too, haven't they?"

Then Miss Carmencita tried to jump off herself, but that didn't work either, because Pippi was holding her tightly around the waist. At that the audience couldn't help laughing. They thought it was funny to see the lovely Miss Carmencita held against her will by a little red-headed youngster who stood there on the horse's back in her enormous shoes and looked as if she had never done anything except perform in a circus.

But the ringmaster didn't laugh. He turned toward an attendant in a red uniform and made a sign to him to go and stop the horse.

"Is this act already over," asked Pippi in a disappointed tone, "just when we were having so much fun?"

"Horrible child!" hissed the ringmaster between his teeth. "Get out of here!"

Pippi looked at him sadly. "Why are you mad at me?" she asked. "What's the matter? I thought we were here to have fun."

She skipped off the horse and went back to her seat.

Meanwhile the next act had begun. It was Miss Elvira about to walk the tightrope. She wore a pink tulle skirt and carried a pink parasol in her hand. With delicate little steps she ran out on the rope. She swung her legs gracefully in the air and did all sorts of tricks. It looked so pretty. She even showed how she could walk backward on the narrow rope. But when she got back to the little platform at the end of the rope, there was Pippi.

"What are you going to do now?" asked Pippi, delighted when she saw how astonished Miss Elvira looked.

Miss Elvira said nothing at all but jumped down from the rope and threw her arms around the ringmaster's neck, for he was her father. The ringmaster

sent for his guards to throw Pippi out, but all the
people shouted, "Let her stay! We want to see the
red-headed girl." And they stamped their feet and
clapped their hands.

Pippi ran out on the rope, and Miss Elvira's tricks
were as nothing compared with Pippi's. When she
got to the middle of the rope she stretched one leg
straight up in the air, and her big shoe spread out
like a roof over her head. She bent her foot a little so
that she could tickle herself with it behind her ear.

The ringmaster was not at all pleased to have
Pippi performing in his circus, so he stole up and
loosened the mechanism that held the rope taut.

But Pippi didn't fall down. She set the rope a-
swinging instead. Back and forth it swayed, and

Pippi swung faster and faster, until suddenly she leaped into the air and landed right on the ringmaster. He was so frightcned he began to run.

Now Pippi decided it was time to go back to Tommy and Annika. She jumped off the ringmaster and went back to her seat. The next act was about to begin, but there was a brief pause because the ringmaster had to go out and get a drink of water and comb his hair.

Then he came in again, bowed to the audience, and said, "Ladies and gentlemen, in a moment you will be privileged to see the Greatest Marvel of all time, the Strongest Man in the World, the Mighty Adolf, whom no one has yet been able to conquer. Here he comes, ladies and gentlemen, Allow me to present to you THE MIGHTY ADOLF."

And into the ring stepped a man who looked as big as a giant. He wore flesh-colored tights and had a leopard skin draped around his stomach. He bowed to the audience and looked very pleased with himself.

"And now, ladies and gentlemen," continued the ringmaster, "I have a very special invitation for you. Who will challenge the Mighty Adolf in a wrestling match? Which of you dares to try his strength against the World's Strongest Man? A hundred dollars for anyone who can conquer the Mighty Adolf! A hundred dollars, ladies and gentlemen! Think of that! Who will be the first to try?"

Nobody came forth.

"What did he say?" asked Pippi.

"He says that anybody who can lick that big man will get a hundred dollars," answered Tommy.

"I can," said Pippi, "but I think it would be too bad to, because he looks nice."

"Oh, no, you couldn't," said Annika, "he's the strongest man in the world."

"*Man*, yes," said Pippi, "but I am the strongest *girl* in the world, remember that."

Meanwhile the Mighty Adolf was lifting heavy iron weights and bending thick iron rods in the middle just to show how strong he was.

"Oh, come now, ladies and gentlemen," cried the ringmaster, "is there really nobody here who wants to earn a hundred dollars? Shall I really be forced to keep this myself?" And he waved a bill in the air.

"No, that you certainly won't be forced to do,"
said Pippi and stepped over the railing into the ring.
She went right up to Mighty Adolf, took his hand,
and shook it heartily.

"Shall we fight a little, you and I?" she asked.

Mighty Adolf just looked at her.

"In one minute I'll begin," said Pippi.

And begin she did. She grabbed Mighty Adolf

around the waist, and before anyone knew what was happening she had thrown him on the mat. Mighty Adolf leaped up, his face absolutely scarlet.

"Atta girl, Pippi!" shrieked Tommy and Annika, so loudly that all the people at the circus heard it and began to shriek, "Atta girl, Pippi!" too.

The ringmaster sat on the railing, wringing his hands. He was mad, but Mighty Adolf was madder. Never in his life had he experienced anything so humiliating as this. And he certainly intended to show that red-headed girl what kind of a man Mighty Adolf really was. He rushed at Pippi and caught her round the waist, but Pippi stood firm as a rock.

"You can do better than that," she said to encourage him. Then she wriggled out of his grasp, and in the twinkling of an eye Mighty Adolf was on the mat again. Pippi stood beside him, waiting. She didn't have to wait long. With a roar he was up again, rushing at her.

"Tiddelipom and piddeliday," said Pippi.

All the people in the tent stamped their feet and threw their hats in the air and shouted, "Hurrah, Pippi!"

When Mighty Adolf came rushing at her for the third time, Pippi lifted him high in the air and, with her arms straight above her, carried him clear

around the ring. Then she laid him down on the mat again and held him there.

"Now, little fellow," said she, "I don't think we'll bother about this any more. We'll never have any more fun than we've had already."

"Pippi is the winner! Pippi is the winner!" cried all the people.

Mighty Adolf stole out as fast as he could, and the ringmaster had to go up and hand Pippi the hundred dollars, although he looked as if he'd much prefer to eat her.

"Here you are, young lady, here you are," he said. "One hundred dollars."

"That thing!" said Pippi scornfully. "What would I want with that old piece of paper. Take it and use it to fry herring on if you want to." And she went back to her seat.

"This is certainly a long surkus," she said to Tommy and Annika. "I think I'll take a little snooze, but wake me if they need my help with anything else."

And then she lay back in her chair and went

to sleep at once. There she lay and snored while the clowns, the sword swallowers, and the snake charmers did their tricks for Tommy and Annika and all the rest of the people at the circus.

"Just the same, I think Pippi was best of all," whispered Tommy to Annika.

The text in this book has been excerpted, with Astrid Lindgren's
assistance, from two chapters in *Pippi Longstocking*.

PUFFIN BOOKS
Published by the Penguin Group
Penguin Putnam Books for Young Readers, 345 Hudson Street, New York, New York 10014, U.S.A.
Penguin Books Ltd, 27 Wrights Lane, London W8 5TZ, England
Penguin Books Australia Ltd, Ringwood, Victoria, Australia
Penguin Books Canada Ltd, 10 Alcorn Avenue, Toronto, Ontario, Canada M4V 3B2
Penguin Books (N.Z.) Ltd, 182-190 Wairau Road, Auckland 10, New Zealand

Penguin Books Ltd, Registered Offices: Harmondsworth, Middlesex, England

First published in the United States of America by Viking,
a member of Penguin Putnam Books for Young Readers, 1999
Published by Puffin Books, a member of Penguin Putnam Books for Young Readers, 2000

5 7 9 10 8 6 4

THE LIBRARY OF CONGRESS HAS CATALOGED THE VIKING EDITION AS FOLLOWS:
Lindgren, Astrid, date
Pippi goes to the circus / by Astrid Lindgren ; illustrated by Michael Chesworth ;
translated by Florence Lamborn.   p. cm.—(A Pippi Longstocking storybook)
Summary: Pippi and her friends, Tommy and Annika, attend the circus where
Pippi walks the tightrope and wrestles with the "World's Strongest Man."
ISBN 0-670-88070-1
[1. Circus—Fiction. 2. Humorous stories. 3. Sweden—Fiction.] I. Chesworth, Michael, ill.
II. Lamborn, Florence. III. Title. IV. Series: Lindgren, Astrid, date, Pippi Longstocking storybook.
PZ7.L6585Pgn 1999 [E]—dc21 98-8836 CIP AC

Puffin Books ISBN 0-14-130243-7

Printed in the United States of America
Set in New Aster